Grison, the Grumpy, Grouchy Island Goat

A Story of Healthy Choices

Carol Schafer

Illustrated by
Alison Schafer Pahl

Carol Schafer

alison Schafer Pahl

GRISON, THE GRUMPY, GROUCHY ISLAND GOAT: A STORY OF HEALTHY CHOICES

ISBN: 978-1-4866-0053-3

Word Alive Press
131 Cordite Road, Winnipeg, MB R3W 1S1
www.wordalivepress.ca

Library and Archives Canada Cataloguing in Publication

Schafer, Carol, 1956-, author
    Grison, the grumpy, grouchy island goat : a story of healthy choices / Carol Schafer ; [illustrated by] Alison Schafer Pahl.
Issued in print and electronic formats.
ISBN 978-1-4866-0053-3 (pbk.).--ISBN 978-1-4866-0054-0 (pdf).--
ISBN 978-1-4866-0055-7 (html).--ISBN 978-1-4866-0056-4 (ebook)

    I. Pahl, Alison Schafer, 1988-, illustrator II. Title.
PS8637.C41G74 2013   jC813'.6   C2013-906130-4
                                               C2013-906131-2

This book belongs to

_____

Part of the royalties from the sale of this book
will be donated to help children in Haiti,
where Grison and other islanders live.

How to say Grison: Gree'-sohn
(It means "greying one.")

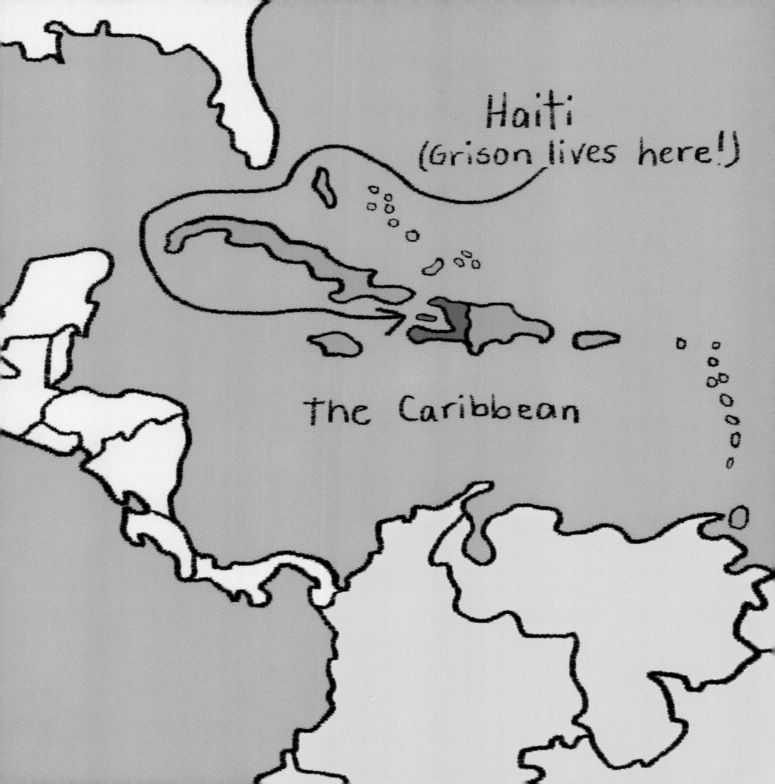

Grison was grouchy. He woke up grouchy in the morning, he was grouchy when the sun shone all day, and he was grouchy when the stars came out at night. He was also grouchy on days when the clouds hung low, and on days when it rained and the wind blew.

Most of the time no one seemed too bothered by Grison's grouchiness. Most of the time the other goats left him alone. Most of the time he liked being left alone.

But sometimes Grison wished the other goats would come around him more. Sometimes they did, but they soon left again. Grison didn't know why, and he was just grumpy about that, too.

When Grison was a much younger goat—a kid goat—he had been bad-tempered. When he played with the other kid goats he kicked them too hard and he butted them too hard. Although young goats sometimes play-kick and play-butt, Grison was bad-tempered, so he took the fighting part of playing too seriously.

While he was growing up, Grison didn't like to do what he was told. If he was told to say please or thank you, he got grouchy. If he was told to tell someone hello, he got grouchy. If he was told to eat his food, he got even more grouchy.

Grison wanted to do things his own way. So he did. He used to be a grouchy young goat. Now he was a grouchy old goat.

Most of the time Grison didn't care. Except for today. Grison was lonely. He also had a stomach ache. He decided to lie on the ground in case that would help. It didn't.

Soon some young goats came near. They were having fun and making a lot of noise. They came closer and closer to where Grison was lying down. And they got noisier, too.

Grison's grouchiness got bigger than his loneliness. "Hey, you kids! Scram!" he shouted. The young goats stopped playing and came even closer.

"I said scram!" Grison shouted again.

"But it's a nice day and we like to play," said one young goat. Her name was Trabelcie, and she was the liveliest of the group. "We'll try not to bother you," she added, remembering to be polite.

"You're already bothering me!" Grison scolded. "Can't you see that I have a stomach ache?"

"Non, Monsieur," said Trabelcie. The young goats all stared at Grison's stomach, but then they shook their heads. They couldn't see that Grison's stomach ached.

"Well, it does," Grison grumbled. "Just leave me alone."

"Tomorrow will be better," Trabelcie said in the cheerful way of islanders.

The kids decided they would have more fun somewhere else. So they left. Grison lay in the same place all day long.

His stomach really did ache. It also growled. Grison was hungry. After a long while, he got up and went to look for something to eat.

A few days later, Grison was snoozing in the shade of a mango tree. Gentle island breezes blew over him, but Grison was restless in his sleep. When he opened his eyes he saw the kids nearby eating the tall grasses.

"Hey, you kids! Scram!" shouted Grison. He was just as grouchy as ever.

The young goats were startled. They had only been munching their favourite grasses. They hadn't been making any noise. Most goats they knew were friendly, but Grison was different than most goats. The kids looked at each other and wondered what to do.

Trabelcie was braver than the others. She stepped closer to Monsieur Grison.

"Still not feeling well, Monsieur? Is it a stomach ache again? Perhaps some of this fresh tall grass will help your stomach ache go away. There's plenty to share." The other kids nodded.

"I said scram!" Grison was cross. "Yes, my stomach aches. And so does my head! Can't you see that my head aches so bad I can't even keep my eyes open?"

The young island goats were sad for Grison. They didn't want him to be sick. They also didn't want him to be grumpy every time they saw him.

"Non, Monsieur," said Trabelcie, "I cannot see that your head aches. Your eyes were closed, it is true, but I thought you were dreaming sweet dreams. I'm sorry that anyone would have a headache on such a lovely day."

Trabelcie really was sorry for Monsieur Grison. She especially thought it must be sad to have a stomach ache *and* a headache.

"Tomorrow will be better," she said cheerily.

9

The island kids weren't hungry anymore, so they left to find something fun to do. This was a good day for exploring the neighbourhood.

Not for Grison, though. He really did have a headache. And he really did have a stomach ache. Grison groaned. After a while, the growling in his stomach got so loud that he dragged himself up to find something to eat.

A few days later, Grison was trying to rest behind an old tire in an alley. The sun was hot. There was no shade. There were no gentle island breezes to cool his body.

Or his temper. Grison was miserable.

As things went, the kids were playing games in the very same alley where Grison was feeling sorry for himself. They stirred up a lot of dust!

Grison was furious! "Hey, you kids! Scram!" he shouted, and he got up from behind the old tire to chase them away.

11

Trabelcie and her friends were dismayed. How come every time they saw Monsieur Grison he was telling them to scram? They were only playing, because that's what kids do. They were not bothering him at all.

"May I ask what is the trouble, Monsieur?" Trabelcie inquired.

"Can't you see that my teeth are hurting?" Grison complained.

"Oh," said Trablecie. "Is your stomach ache gone yet?"

"No."

"Is your headache gone yet?"

"No."

The other kids stood by. They didn't like being in trouble with Monsieur Grison. They didn't know why he was always so grumpy with them. They wished he would feel better so everyone could be happy and have fun together.

So, in the cheerful way of islanders, Trabelcie said, "Tomorrow will be better, Monsieur."

"I doubt it," Grison replied.

Then Trabelcie noticed something odd. She stared at Monsieur Grison. He didn't like that.

"Scram, kid," he muttered.

But Trabelcie stared even more. "You said your teeth hurt, Monsieur?"

The other kids were staring now, too. Grison could feel his temper rising. Then Trabelcie twitched her nose and stepped closer. Grison stepped back. Trabelcie stepped closer again. Grison stepped back again.

"Monsieur Grison," said Trabelcie, as though she were about to deliver an important message, "you have a piece of wire sticking out of your mouth. Why do you have wire in your mouth? Do you have a piece of wire stuck between your teeth?" Trabelcie couldn't stop staring at Monsieur Grison's mouth.

"Scram, kid," Grison grumbled, and he turned away. "And mind your own business."

Trabelcie couldn't help but wonder why anyone would have a piece of wire in their mouth. Goats don't eat wire. They eat grass. Lots of kinds of grasses. Wonderful, yummy grasses. Eating wire would make any goat sick!

In the way of the most clever island goats, Trabelcie had an idea.

"Goodbye, Monsieur," she said. "Tomorrow will be better."

The kids all left, so Grison grumbled to himself. He truly did have a stomach ache. He truly did have a headache. He truly did have a toothache. And he truly did have a piece of wire sticking out of his mouth!

Grison lay behind the old tire for a long time. Later, when the growling in his

stomach got so loud he couldn't hear himself think, he got up to find something to eat.

Grison took his usual path down the alley, around the corner, around another corner, and then one more, and up behind the wall to his favourite place to eat.

17

Grison looked around.
He found a bit of this.

A bite of that.

A few chunks of something crunchy.

And leftovers of something chewy.

He finished off with something soft and squishy.

Grison was thirsty, so he looked around for something to drink. He found something sweet and sticky, and he slurped it up. And then he burped.

"Excuse me," he said, even though no one was around.

"You're excused," came a voice from behind the grasses.

Grison turned to see who had spoken to him.

"Scram, kid! I don't like anyone around when I'm eating."

"Eating?" said Trabelcie. She had followed him all the way. She had watched him eat all kinds of junk. "But where is your food, Monsieur?"

"Scram, kid!" Grison said again, but this time he sounded a little embarrassed. "I can eat whatever I feel like eating."

"But this is not food for island goats," Trabelcie insisted. "Island goats eat the tall grasses. And the short grasses. And the yummy green grasses. I did not see you eating them, Monsieur."

"Scram, kid!" Grison was losing his patience. "I can eat wherever I feel like eating."

Trabelcie said nothing. She was thinking. She was also remembering. Monsieur Grison had been grumpy and grouchy as long as she could remember. He always seemed to be feeling sick. He always seemed to be unhappy. Trabelcie didn't remember ever seeing Monsieur Grison eat with the other island goats. Not even once!

Could it be? she wondered. *Could it be that Monsieur Grison always comes here to eat? Does he always eat at the junkyard? Does he always eat junk food at the junkyard?*

That would be unhealthy. Unsanitary. Unwise. And completely absurd!

"Monsieur Grison," Trabelcie said carefully, "I think I know how you can stop having such bad stomach aches."

Grison ignored her as he licked something greasy.

"And I think I know how you can stop having such bad headaches," Trabelcie continued.

Grison ignored her as he chewed on something hard and crunchy.

"And I think I know how you can stop having toothaches," Trabelcie said quickly. She knew she was being bold. Maybe too bold. After all, Monsieur Grison didn't like anyone telling him anything. Especially not a kid like her!

Grison lifted his head. He scowled at Trabelcie. He wanted to tell her to scram—but he couldn't say anything! His teeth were stuck together! Grison's teeth were stuck in a great big wad of something sticky and gooey!

24

Trabelcie took a deep breath. "Monsieur Grison, you do not feel well because you do not eat well. If you want to feel well, you will need to make healthy choices.

"But you are correct, Monsieur. You can eat whatever and wherever you wish. But I wish that you would make healthy choices about your food. And I wish that you would feel better and enjoy each day. And I really wish you could become friends with the other island goats. And I wish that tomorrow will be better."

Trabelcie backed away. "And now, I guess I should scram, huh?" she said in a sad whisper.

Grison didn't say anything. His teeth were still stuck together! He watched as Trabelcie wandered off into the darkness on her way home.

Is it true? Grison wondered that night as he lay in the junkyard. *Is it true that I can feel better? Is it possible for a grumpy, grouchy old island goat to change his ways?* Grison didn't know. He thought about that for a long time as he tried to get his teeth unstuck.

Finally, long into the night, Grison could open his mouth again. He was so exhausted that he just lay there with his tongue hanging out.

Then Grison had an idea. He didn't know if it would work. He had been a grumpy, grouchy old island goat for so long that he didn't know if he could change at all. But he had to know the truth for himself.

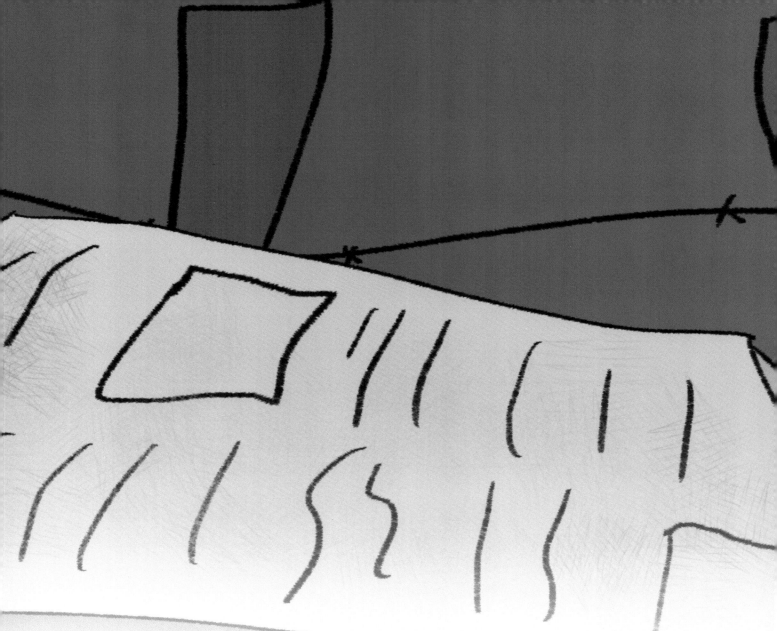

While the night sky was still black, Grison got up and scuffled around the junkyard, looking for something useful. He didn't want to be recognized by any of the other island goats. But he had to know if Trabelcie was right about the tall grasses and the short grasses. Grison needed a disguise.

Then he shuffled out of the junkyard, back around the wall,

around a corner, and then another corner,

across the road, through the ditch,

and over to the *shady green place where the tallest grasses grew.*

Grison shuddered at the thought of eating green food, but he remembered Trabelcie's words and he had to know if the grasses were truly yummy.

Grison took a bite. The grasses felt cool in his mouth. He started to chew. The grasses were crunchy. The cool and crunchy grasses tasted good. They really were yummy!

When Grison had finished sampling a variety of tall grasses he nibbled on some short grasses. Then he wandered around, tasting more tall and short grasses. He kept eating. He didn't even know that the sun had come up. That is, he didn't know it until the gentle island breeze turned into a blustery gust of wind. Grison's disguise was caught in the wind and lifted high into the air!

The other island goats noticed the newspaper flying over their heads. Then they noticed Grison. Some looked away quickly, thinking that Grison would say something cross to them, but not Trabelcie.

Trabelcie noticed that Monsieur Grison looked different. Very different. He had yummy green grasses in his mouth!

"Bonjour, Monsieur." Trabelcie scampered over to greet him.

"Bonjour," Grison answered quietly.

Monsieur Grison hadn't told her to scram! Instead, he was talking to her!

"Would you care to join me for breakfast?" Grison asked. He was shy, but he really wanted to be friendly. "The tall grasses are especially fresh and yummy this morning."

Trabelcie watched as Monsieur Grison's mouth twitched. It was as though he was happy! Monsieur Grison wanted to smile!

"It would be a great honour to join you for breakfast today, Monsieur." Trabelcie's smile was brighter than the morning sun. "Perhaps you are feeling better today, Monsieur? And perhaps we could even be friends?"

Grison smiled his biggest smile ever. "Perhaps," he said softly, "today is going to be a good day." And then, in the cheerful way of islanders, he said, "And tomorrow will be even better!"

This is the day the LORD has made.
We will rejoice and be glad in it.
(Psalm 118:24, NLT)

CPSIA information can be obtained
at www.ICGtesting.com
Printed in the USA
LVIW02n0041101113
360424LV00001B/2